DIAMOND'S DELIGHT

A MOORE SISTERS STORY II

The Moore Sisters of Center City

Angelia Vernon Menchan

Honorable MENCHAN Media L.L.C. 2022

2

Diamond woke up grinning. The sun shone bright through her windows and her body was relaxed. She decided to ask Keith to spend the night after several weeks of dating and it was everything and more. He was passionate, all about her pleasure and held her on his big chest *after* the sex. She wasn't calling it anything but what it was. A great time with a big, sexy, good-looking man.

A huge grin covered her face when she saw a full pot of coffee and her *Diamond's Delights* mug sitting next to the pot. There was a note.

I saw all the work laid out and figured you would need a little something, something. I know you got the cakes on lock.
KEITH.

3

She grinned because she loved him writing his name in big, cold caps. Big and bold like him.

You've come a long way baby. She sang as she danced around her kitchen. Her counter was filled with cake flour, vanilla, lemon and coconut extracts, lemons and other flavors. There was a bowl filled with butter and another with cream cheese she had danced over to take out of the refrigerator to come to room temperature. It was cake baking day. Her small business *Diamond's Delights* was booming thanks to her skills, the support of her sister Crystal and Crystal's man, the one and only Messiah, R&B sensation. Messiah had turned out to be the humblest man she ever met. But—Keith was the sexiest.

CHAPTER ONE

The first cakes were cooling when Diamond's daughters Opal and Emerald trudged in the house grumbling with each other. They spent the night with Rose, Diamond's middle sister but came home to eat before school.

Opal was thirteen but seemed older due to her height and blooming figure. Diamond wasn't allowing her to wear makeup yet but still. Emerald at eleven was shorter and plump with a baby face and loved her mama, books and food in that order. Opal was a good student, Emerald excelled in her classes.

6

"Y'all better stop all that fussing. There are baked pancakes with bacon in the top oven." Diamond said and the girls gave each other looks but didn't say anything else to each other. Opal grabbed her warm plate and sat at the table, flipping her braids over her shoulder. Emerald kissed her mom's face before grabbing her food, making Opal mutter something.

"Opal." Diamond warned.
The girls ate quietly while Diamond sipped her second cup of coffee. After their breakfast she took out the second batch of cakes to cool and took them to school. Opal wanted to take the bus but that was a no for Diamond. She took them and picked them up or Rose or Crystal picked them up.

"Mom, surely I'll be allowed to ride the bus to high school." Opal whined.

"What makes you so sure, Ms. Opal, did I say that?"

"No ma'am." Opal mumbled. Emerald snickered under her breath.

"Emerald, stay out my business." Opal said.

"You ain't got no business." Emerald retorted.

"Both of y'all going to get the business if you don't stop. You know you don't want it." Diamond said. They rolled their eyes at each other but shut it down. Emerald kissed her mom's face at the school, but Opal jumped out of the car, rushing to her friends.

"It's okay mama, it's not you it's puberty." Emerald said. Diamond held back a snort. She remembered her own puberty.

"Have a good day, Emerald."

"Yes ma'am. You too."

Diamond watched Emerald walk past Opal and her friends to a group of kids near the school door. She saw them engage as she pulled away. Opal had always been popular, but Emerald was finally coming into her own in sixth grade. She had been a shy, chubby, brainy kid who loved books which didn't make for popularity. Middle school exposed her to more kids like her. Emerald except for being chubby reminded Diamond of her youngest sister Crystal. Crystal was a quiet overachiever as well.

That thickness is all on me. Diamond thought, smiling.

¥¥¥¥¥

Her heart was pounding in her chest when Diamond pulled up to the nondescript building. It was a house that had been transformed into a real estate office. She hadn't said anything to anyone, not even Crystal but she was getting assistance with purchasing a home. Since incorporating her business, she felt it was time. She was qualified for several funding programs as a single mom and small business owner. She was starting the process. It felt *powerful* to have a check for five thousand dollars, money she earned, doing what she loved as her down payment.

At the end of the class Diamond went into the restroom and danced a jig. She was eligible for a four-bedroom home for her and her girls. It was being refurbished and had a nice lot. She was going to tell the girls and Crystal later at dinner. She invited Rose and her girls, but Rose declined after hearing Crystal was coming.

¥¥¥¥¥

"When are we meeting this woman, you've been seeing?" Keith Sr., Keith's father asked. "KJ said you've been out."

Keith and his son KJ were having dinner with his parents. Keith Sr. and Vera were retired custodians in their early sixties and loved their son and grandson. Since Keith got custody, they assisted and loved them every step of the way. It was a blessing because KJ was high-functioning autistic. KJ was grinning at his dad who winked at him.

"I have been out. Her name is Diamond, and she has two daughters. She has a small business and I hooked up her website. I like her—a lot."

Keith Sr. nodded and glanced at his wife. "Dad, why you looking at mom, she made her choice with you? I'm good on making my choices." Keith Sr. rumbled with laughter. That's exactly what he said to Vera when she said something to him after KJ said he was dating. Vera's mouth tightened a bit, but Keith always made clear his business was his unless he invited them in. She had gotten overly involved when Keith was with KJ's mother and Keith had to tell her to back off.

"I always look at your mom son. She's pretty and been my boo for nearly forty years but you right. We raised a man, a good man. We would love to meet her. I can't speak for Vera, but I'll be on my best behavior." Vera rolled

13

her eyes sending Keith Sr. on another round of laughter.

"Man hush." Vera said. At sixty-three, she was a pretty woman with unlined mocha skin and a fit well-padded figure. She kept in shape by walking and gardening. "And Keith, you have made it clear where my lane is and I'm in it."

"Mom, I'm the man who models the man you love and chose as my dad." Keith said. "Blame your husband."

"Oh, she does." Keith Sr. said, his eyes filled with humor.

"Grandma said Walker men a mess and think their sh…" KJ started but Vera yelled his name and he stopped. Keith and his dad exchanged looks before laughing gleefully. Vera's nose was flared.

"My bad." KJ said. His tone nonchalant. To Keith that was the beauty of his son, he was genuinely honest because he didn't know how not to be. KJ was an excellent student and artistic, but his sometimes-uncontrollable honesty didn't always go well with his peers or elders. Also, if you said something around him, he was likely to repeat it. Saying exactly what he thought was the main way his autism manifested.

"KJ she's right, we are confident and can be a mess, but we are good, hardworking men who love their women and children. I'll take us over a lot of them." Keith said. Keith Sr. proudly nodded in agreement. He knew his wife as loving, protective and faithful but that loving protectiveness could be meddlesome and overbearing. He raised Keith to not be manipulated by his mom.

Son, your mom loves us more than anyone, but she has a strong desire to control what she loves. She will go further than you allow every time until you stop it. You chose that girl, it's up to you to unchoose her, not Vera. I'm not gon tell you your mama's business but she's not always been the woman she is.

At the time Keith was a twenty-four-year-old with a son from a girlfriend ten years older and a bonafide split personality. Vera hated her on first sight and spoke badly about her in front of his then three-year-old son. That was the day he had to tell her what her lane was, and he reminded her periodically to stay in it. It's also why he gave her monetary *gifts* for the time she took care KJ when he was younger. Paying, even family members, kept the lines clear.

"When it's meeting time, I'll let everyone know." Keith said. "Or I'll tell KJ." KJ's eyes widened at his dad's remark. Keith held KJ accountable and never allowed him excuses. KJ nodded in understanding. Their therapist advised Keith to reinforce things to KJ even if it didn't work every time.

"KJ did you get your cake?" Vera asked. KJ didn't like candy or cookies like many kids. The only sweets he ate was Vera's cakes and she baked him one every week.

"No ma'am. We have a lot of cake. Daddy's friend is *Diamond's Delights*. It's great too." He said. Keith cringed at the look that flickered across Vera's face. In his perpetual innocence KJ wounded Vera. Those cakes were their bond. "I'm going to get it now though, it's my favorite." He said and ambled off to get it. Keith embraced Vera and kissed her forehead.

"Got my baby cheating on my cakes." She said. Keith heard the humor in her voice and the hurt.

"Vera Walker, we would never cheat on your cakes. You were putting that cake in our bottles. It's why we so big and healthy." Keith hit his middle for emphasis but though he was a big guy his stomach was hard and muscular.

"Only fools cheat, grandma." KJ said, walking in with his backpack and cake securely wrapped in foil. Vera's mouth flew open, and Keith was stunned. Neither said *that* in front of him. It hit Keith that his son was growing up, becoming a man. Because he hadn't had to deal with the usual teen concerns such as girls and getting into trouble, he often forgot KJ just turned sixteen. Keith stared at the growing man who looked just like him and was as tall but much slimmer with an easier smile. His heart thrummed with love for his son. Keith Sr. looked on smiling.

Our KJ is on his way to manhood. Keith Sr. thought.

"You good dad?" KJ asked.

"Umm, yea, let's ride."

"Our kid raised a good kid." Keith Sr. said. Vera sucked her teeth but acknowledged what her husband said. Keith was a good man and raised a good kid. "Next thing you know KJ will be driving around with him a honey who bakes."

Vera threw up her middle finger and left the kitchen. Keith Sr.'s chuckled followed her.

Let his ass clean up.

She's as fiery as ever. Keith Sr. thought as he rolled up his shirt sleeves to wash dishes and clean the kitchen.

Vera was looking up Diamond's cakes on the internet. Perusing every page and cake. She was hoping to see the woman, but the only image was the cartoon design Opal created.

CHAPTER TWO

The house was spotless, but Diamond checked and re-checked everything. They were raised by Elaine to be almost obsessively clean, but she had to admit having Messiah come to dinner added pressure. She knew he wasn't that guy, but it mattered to her.

"You're real." Opal said when introduced to Messiah. Her eyes were huge in her face. Diamond noticed she looked like her little girl again and not the perpetually bored teen she was becoming. Emerald on the other hand said, "welcome, my mom makes the bomb macaroni and cheese."

"Even more bomb than her lemon curd cream cheesecake?" Messiah asked sounding skeptical. Placing her forefinger on her face, Emerald appeared to be thinking deeply about it.

"Hmm, you might have me there." Emerald said and even Opal laughed.

After his second serving, Messiah pushed back his chair and faced Emerald.

"Ms. Emerald, I think it's a tie because that macaroni and cheese was the bomb. I wonder if your Auntie can cook macaroni and cheese like that?" Diamond and her girls chuckled; Crystal rolled her eyes.

"I don't know Mr. Messiah because the Moore ladies stay in their lanes. Only mom makes the cakes and macaroni and cheese, Aunt Rose kills crabs and stuff but fried chicken and hot wings, Auntie Crystal is the winner. Grandma says a cook should always know her place." Messiah laughed from deep in his gut. Crystal kissed her teeth and pointed her finger at Emerald.

"Oh yeah, grandma just came to eat. Our great grandma taught mama and the aunties how to cook." Opal interjected and that brought sister hand slaps. Messiah couldn't stop grinning, there wasn't much he loved more than seeing family communication. That was something his brother and sister taught him, how to love and snap on each other.

"When Crystal takes me to meet your grandma maybe I'll find out." Messiah said slyly and all eyes turned to Diamond, except his. He stared off not meeting her eyes, a comical expression on his face.

"Okay Messiah, I see you but don't say nothing when you try to swallow that dry chicken and dressing thing she loves to make. Not oven that heated up mushroom soup helps it." Crystal said. Diamond almost choked laughing, the girls were clapping in agreement.

"That bad, huh?" Messiah asked. Everyone yelled yes in agreement.

Diamond spotted Rose sitting on the porch when they walked outside with Messiah and Crystal. The girls were fully enamored of Messiah and they and Crystal were thrilled about their new home. Messiah had sung karaoke with them, allowing them to record his voice and theirs. Crystal waved and Rose turned her head. The girls glanced at their mom who shrugged.

"Baby, we can walk down there." Messiah said softly to Crystal. Diamond swallowed a lump at the sweetness of the gesture. Crystal shook her head before hugging Diamond and the girls.

"He's so in love with TT." Opal said dreamily watching them drive away.

"Duh, TT the bomb." Emerald said.

"I'm going to sit on the steps, y'all get the kitchen squared away." Diamond said. Her phone buzzed as she sat. A smile covered her face when she saw Keith's number.

"Hey."

"Hey, how was the dinner?

"It was great. The girls and my sister were happy about the new house." Keith was the only person Diamond mentioned the house to until everything was settled. That surprised her but he was easy to talk to.

"That's dope. I want to invite you and the girls to my place for dinner. I need to meet them, and I want y'all to meet KJ." A frisson of pleasure filled Diamond's belly. She told the girls about Keith and his son.

"I would like that. When?" Keith pumped his fist in the air.

"Sunday, I know it's in two days…"

"Sunday is good, I've got dessert."

"I hope you bring cake too cause that dessert is mine." Shards of painful desire shot through her because the last time he ate *that* cake she almost lost her mind.

"I got you." She whispered.

"I like that. I'll call you later. Tell the girls KJ speaks without being able to filter some things. He's getting better but it's part of who he is."

"Keith, my youngest child is the same without a diagnosis. They will be fine. Talk later." She hung up smiling, still staring at her phone.

"Guess that's your man." Rose's voice filtered through Diamond's thoughts but couldn't alter how she felt about the house, the dinner and Keith.

"I think he might be." Diamond said simply. Rose's nose flared but she sat two steps down from her sister. Diamond wasn't going to tell Rose about the house yet and told the girls not to say a word. "Where is Amber and Ebony?"

"With Reggie, of course." Diamond heard something almost melancholy in Rose's voice. The girls preferred being there, Reggie and his mom spoiled them, and Rose was always mad about something. "Your sister looks good—I guess dating suits her."

"Rose, she's, our sister. Messiah is a good, good man."

Rose lifted her cup and took a deep sip of her cocktail.

"They're all good until they ain't. I know you made me a pan of macaroni and cheese."

"Heffa, you know I did. It's on the table next to your cake." Rose rolled her eyes, but a hint of a smile was in her eyes changing her face. The door opened and Emerald walked out with a bag for Rose. She sat on the step next to her.

"TT today was fun. We recorded music with Mr. Messiah. Opal in there singing to it now. You can't tell her she's not a good singer." Emerald said and leaned onto Rose's shoulder. Emerald and Amber were the same age, Amber four months older. Rose winked at her niece but didn't say anything. Diamond swallowed a lump, Emerald always tried being a peacemaker.

"I'm going home to eat my macaroni and cheese without my greedy children." Rose said, standing and grabbing her bag. Diamond and Emerald watched her walk away.

"She's sad mommy."

"I know baby. I learned we must choose happy. Let's go eat some cake *and* ice cream."

¥¥¥¥¥

Crystal stared out the window as they drove along the coast. After leaving Diamond's Messiah suggested a drive; Crystal gladly accepted.

"Baby, we could have walked down there." Messiah said. "I could see you wanted to." Crystal turned in her sat to face him.

"I did but Rose is hard and if she feels pushed, she squares off. I'm used to her, but I didn't want her insulting you." A look of surprise covered Messiah's face, but the warmth of her words touched him.

"You were concerned about me? I'm good, I've seen and heard most things. I'm a black man, my mom lied to me about my parentage, I dated a married woman, and some folks tell me to my face my music is trash. So, what if Rose insulted me, were you going to take her down?"

"I might have." Crystal said. Messiah's crotch tightened at her words.

"I'm almost ashamed to admit how damn hot that sounded."
She poked out her lips before licking them.
"Let someone mess with you, they will get it."

"Damn..."

"Sing about that Messiah, *Mess Wit Me, Deal Wit My Woman.*"

"Keep talking that shit Crystal, you the one gon get it."

"Then I shall, cause I want it." She said, narrowing her eyes and biting her lip.

The lyrics to the song started filling his brain as his erection threatened to tear open his pants.

"Next exit, we heading to the hotel!" He said.

Her sensual laughter filled the car.

CHAPTER THREE

The girls ran around in the yard, screaming, even Opal.

So, a new house and her TT's crooner brings out the kid in my kid. Diamond thought watching them. She brought them to see the house before dinner with Keith and KJ. The look on their faces as she showed them the house was everything. For too long fear ruled her, kept her from starting a business, wanting more and even from dating. But seeing her sister at Christmas and earning ten thousand dollars baking cakes in less than six weeks was also helpful. Cakes were her creation and she loved it. Until Crystal encouraged her, she was giving them away or underselling them. It was hard because most days she created twenty cakes, there was even a fifty-cake day, but she would *never* do that again. The idea she needed to hire someone freaked her out.

"Come on girls." She yelled and watched them race to the car.

¥¥¥¥¥

"Wo, his house is huge." Opal said as they pulled onto Keith's property, and it was a property. The house sat on three acres and there were lots of trees and beautiful grass. The house wasn't massive but was bigger than the house of anyone they knew. Keith told Diamond he purchased the property for four thousand dollars and lived in a house trailer that cost half that until he and his friends built the stone home he wanted. He told her about growing up in the projects but his parents saving and moving him out before he was a teen. He also told them Keith Sr. told him to do well in school, always have more than one way to earn money and buy something of his own. She smiled remembering that conversation.

He also told me to get me a fine, thick woman who can cook and likes to eat." She had giggled like a teen.

"Mom!"

"Huh?"

"We're here and you're looking weird." Opal said.

"Girl hush and get out of my car." Diamond said, opening her door and getting out. Emerald raced to knock but the door opened. Keith and KJ waved them in, looking like large and extra-large bookends.

"Welcome to our home Ms. Diamond. Also, Opal and Emerald. Wow, three jewels." KJ said. "I'm KJ and dad told me not to look too hard at your daughters or you because of my raging hormones." Keith groaned at KJ saying exactly what he told him not to and the howling laughter that came out of Diamond's mouth.

"KJ, thank you. You are something good." Diamond finally said. Opal looked skeptical. Of course, Emerald had something to say, "KJ, you will be fine. Mom's old and I'm a little kid, if you just ignore my sister everything will be good." It was Keith's turn to laugh out loud.

"Whatever Emerald." Opal said, tossing her braids.

"Okay, let me show y'all where the restrooms are. We out back cooking." Keith said. KJ pulled on headphones and Opal was on her phone.

'Out back' was a room-sized covered patio, fully furnished with an outdoor kitchen and a unending backyard. There were also three hammocks which the kids immediately got in.

"Your home is beautiful Keith."

Diamond and Keith were sitting on the patio. He was drinking a beer, but she told him she couldn't drink when she was driving. Even if hours passed, it was a risk she wasn't willing to take. Especially with her girls in the car. He respected and understood that.

"Thank you. It took me four years to build it. I was and then we were in a small trailer until it was done. I paid as I built. I love it out here, it's only twenty minutes from Center City but feels further. It's great for my kid." They both glanced towards the kids and saw KJ reading Emerald's book and her drawing in a pad he gave her. Opal was on her phone.

"He's a special kid." Diamond said, watching the kids.

"He is. He's smart, funny and kind. But he's behind in things such as socializing because of his inability to filter. It's a mixed blessing because at sixteen it was girls, girls, girls for me and other stupid stuff. I see women and girls eyeing him because of how he looks but socially he's very young. But he tests off the charts and will graduate a year early from high school." Diamond loved listening to Keith. He was laid back, earnest and honest.

She'd never met a man like him. He was thirty-seven but he had a wise, old-school vibe.

"Did you spend a lot of time with your dad growing up?" Diamond asked. A huge smile suffused his face.

"I did and do. Keith Sr. is an amazing dad. I want that for KJ. He will be with me longer than most kids and I'm good with it. Where is the girls' father, any involvement?"

"He's in Jacksonville. They rarely hear from him and even more rarely do they see him. He got kicked out of the Navy up there and stayed. He works odd jobs under the table and sends a few dollars here and there. I

released him from child-support years ago."
Keith listened and kept his opinion on dads
who didn't take care of their kids to himself.
He held them in the lowest regard. "At one
time Gary was a decent guy. I was twenty and
working in Jacksonville at Mayport when I
met him. He drank a lot but was fun and from
Detroit, city slick. I was enamored and had
two babies in three years. He got kicked out
of the service when Emerald was a baby. I
brought my girls home to The Gardens
because he refused to work and was always
drinking. He's the reason I won't take a sip of
alcohol and drive my girls."

"It was similar with KJ's mom and I but she
was ten years older. Turned my ass out. She
was a fun drunk too but was mean as a snake

other times. I found out she was mentally unstable and tried to stick it out, but it was— she was too much. I'm grateful she gave me my son."

They grew quiet and Keith got up to get the food off the smoker and yelled for the kids to wash up to eat.

"Mr. Keith you cook great." Emerald said, barbecue sauce on her face. They were eating at a big picnic table.

"Thank you. What do you think Opal?" Keith asked. Opal had only eaten small bites of the steak and sausage. She hadn't gotten any bread, corn or grilled beans.

"It's good." She murmured. "I don't eat much." Emerald snorted and ate another bite of sausage.

"You eat a lot, but you think thin is beautiful." KJ said. "It isn't, it's just thin. You need more flesh, not as much as your mom but more." Keith inhaled, holding his breath.

"Boy!" Opal said scraping her chair back and getting out of her chair. Her stance was fight ready.

Keith looked on, his eyes on Diamond, he was concerned about her reaction. There was no real preparation for KJ except being around him. He was surprised that Diamond's head was thrown back in laughter. Tears ran from her eyes.

"Opal, sit down. You know you ain't ready for curves like this and KJ you are alright with me. I love it." Diamond said. Opal rolled her eyes giving KJ a look and shaking her fist at him. He looked unimpressed but Keith was staring at Diamond. He wanted to kiss her until her lips were raw. Instead, he cleared his throat.

"KJ, you're saying a lot son." Keith admonished his voice stern.

"Too much, dad?"

"Way too much." Opal interjected. "Talking about Diamond Moore will get you hurt. We don't play about her."

Diamond felt the fierce protectiveness of her daughter's words. They were currently driving each other crazy but they had each other, always.

"My bad Ms. Diamond, you are very pretty but you are thick." KJ said.

Keith could only close his eyes. Diamond placed her head on the table laughing hard; harder than she laughed in years.

"KJ, I'm going to help you with your social skills. For real." Emerald said. "Mr. Keith, I'll send you my bill because this boy got to learn.”

“I’ll pay good.” Keith said, still watching Diamond who was wiping her eyes. KJ grinned charmingly at Emerald.

“Y’all have delighted me today.” Diamond said. “That’s on everything. After I use the restroom we will have my new cake, peach cobbler pound cake.” She got up and went to the restroom still chuckling. Keith wanted to follow her but restrained himself.

¥¥¥¥¥

“Today was good?” Keith asked Diamond later at the door. The girls were gathering their things. KJ had said his goodbyes and was in his room.

"It was the best day I had in—a long time. KJ is fine as he is. The world needs more like him."

Keith pulled her close and lightly kissed her forehead. He wanted to lick her face and bite her neck.

"Can we have an alone night soon?" He asked, his voice husky.

"Yea, Friday is good."

"Until Friday Delightful Diamond." They heard the girls and stepped apart.

"Thanks Mr. Keith." Emerald said. Opal had her bored face back on.

"Mr. Keith what I told KJ goes for everyone, we don't play about our mama." Opal said. Keith folded his hands in front of him and bowed his head.

"I promise you I'm no player Ms. Opal." He walked out with them.

That's my woman. He thought. *Or she will be.*

"That KJ's a trip." Opal said once they were in the car.

"He can't help it, Opal. That's why *I* gave him a pass. He's very nice." Emerald said.

"Umm hmm, I'm watching him."

Diamond didn't say anything, but she wanted to hug her girls and KJ. And ride Keith's lap.

CHAPTER FOUR

The Thursday after the dinner at Keith's, Diamond finally had a free day. It was time to talk to her sister—Rose. She wrapped her newest creation and made the short walk. Rose was on her porch people watching as usual, perfectly coiffed and made up dressed in lavender sweats, her favorite color and attire.

Diamond handed Rose the still warm cake and sat next to her on a swing.

"Well damn, if it isn't big sister coming to my house. Ain't no cakes baking?"

"Rose don't start your shit. You know I grind and the minute I walk outside you come to my house. I *am* the big sister."

"Word is you moving, so that won't be a thing much longer." Rose said. Her voice was its usual dry sarcasm.

"Who told you?"

"You didn't. Reggie told me. You know he reads the papers and is always on city websites. Was it a secret?" Rose asked, finally looking at her sister.

"No, that was the point of the dinner you missed. Truth is Ro it's hard to tell you anything. You've blasted on Crys for years and barely speak to mama since she moved. You're never happy for anyone." Diamond said and exhaled. It needed saying even if Rose cut her off too. "So, I'm telling you now. In three months, the girls and I are moving.

"That might be true, but I love the hood and I can't stand those who have to leave to make it."

"So, you seriously can't stand a lot of folks." Diamond said drily. The door opened and Reggie the girls father rolled out in his custom wheelchair. He was a slim, handsome man with massive shoulders and medium brown skin who always wore spotless white sneakers and ball caps.

"Diamond, you know your sister don't want to do nothing and be mad at everybody who do. But we gonna love her but still do us." He said. A car pulled up and Reggie rolled down the ramp he had installed to his ride.

He's absolutely right. Diamond thought.

"I was going to ask if you wanted to help me with orders sometimes, for pay of course but being you can't stand me…" Diamond said as she stood to leave. She threw Rose a glance before walking down the steps and home.

¥¥¥¥¥

Three hours later Diamond heard pounding on her door. She had fallen asleep in her chair after returning home. Crystal was picking up the girls after school and taking them to visit aquariums and museums Friday and Saturday. Friday was a school holiday and Crystal was off. She also invited Rose's girls but got no answer.

Diamond rushed to the door only to see Rose sitting on her step. She went to the restroom and washed her face before grabbing a bottle of water and going outside.

"Rose, I don't have any more cake…"

"How much were you going to pay me and what would I be doing?" Rose asked in her typical fashion, pretending as if nothing occurred earlier.

"Why?" Diamond wasn't trying to make it easier for her sister. She sat on the steps above Rose as she had for years.

"I might be interested. Just to help you and all."

"It pays fifteen dollars an hour. I need about fifteen hours a week, more if I have special orders."

"I guess I can help you but don't take no tax out of my money."

"Woman please. This is legitimate, ain't like you got any other viable income. Take it or leave it."

"I'll try it. Reggie's on your side. He called talking about I better be nice to you and him, y'all the only two grown folks who still talk to me. I cussed his ass out."

But you heard him and here you are. Diamond thought.

"I'm sure Reggie has heard it all before. He loves you and it's real because he *knows* you and still shows up." Rose held up her middle finger at her sister but there was a hint of a smile on her face.

The truth was she called Reggie to vent about Diamond, but he went off.

Ro, you are going to be all alone you keep on with your shit. You barely talk to your mama; you haven't talked to your brother or Crystal in years, and you mean as hell to me. Diamond might be your last straw. That's your ace and she's always been there when everyone else was out. You might want to slide your mean ass down there and make it right. Ain't nobody done nothing to you. They are all the realest people and especially Crystal. Folks just trying to get their money and have something. Get your mind right before my kids be just like you. She had cussed him out but like Diamond said he heard it all before. He laughed *and* hung up. It took her two more hours to walk to Diamond's house, but she did.

"What am doing at this gig?"

"Helping me ice cakes that need icing and lots of packaging and there will be some cleaning." Rose was the cleaning queen; they were all taught to clean, but Rose was other level.

"I can get with that. I'm no baker as you know but I can package and clean better than most."

"That's why I want you. Sometimes I need delivery help also."

Rose spun around to face her sister fully. She could see the relaxation in her sister's expression. She knew part of it was good sex after a long drought but had to admit owning a business was a big part of it.

"Being a boss and getting some D looks good on you." Rose said. Diamond giggled girlishly. "Reggie said Keith a real one."

"You say, Reggie said a lot."

"He says a lot." Rose said and busted out laughing. Her rare infectious laughter made Diamond laugh too.

"True. Always running his mouth but if you pay attention, he makes sense most of the time."

"Every time except the times he doesn't. Nobody can have you believing ridiculous shit like Reggie. His mama just as bad."

"You fit right in. You *thee* trash talking Moore sister." Rose moved her hand like she was waving away Diamond's words.

"Whatever. Reggie wants us to move in. He got five bedrooms over there, but I need my privacy."

Diamond kept mum. She couldn't see Rose and Reggie's Mom Lisa living in the same house, no matter how big it was. They were both moody, loved to drink and argue. They also competed for Reggie's attention.

"But you know me, and Lisa cannot. I'm good."

"Can you start Monday? I got thirty cakes to bake Sunday. Most are pound cakes."

"Wo, that's real."

"It tis. Having Messiah on #TeamDiamond is a thing."

"I bet. Monday is good. I never aspired to any of that Diamond." Diamond tuned in fully. It was rare for Rose to share beyond the surface.

"Any of what Rose?"

"Careers, men like Keith, much less like Messiah. I remember, our brother was a spoiled boy, you were the big sister who could cook like a chef and the boys loved you because you were pretty and *fine—fine* like Mama. I was the sister who could clean and fight, cute but skinny. Then along came Crystal and from day one that was Mama's baby and yours. She was beautiful, even finer than you once she grew up and outworked everyone and was so damn good, I couldn't stand her." Rose paused and Diamond swallowed a lump, she couldn't deny any of that. "But the Reggies of the world loved me, I was that chick to them, and I loved that. I still don't aspire to any of it, I like my duplex, I got bank—I been saving since Reggie was in the streets and giving me a bag. No one ever understands we ain't all trying to be world changers. If I decide to move, I'll move but believe me big sis, I'm good—for now. You and me, we will always be good, D, you're big sis."

Diamond felt her sister's words deeply and knew it took a lot for her to say it.

"I love your grumpy butt too. I also love your little speech, but I'll always want more for you —and Crystal. I'm also getting what I want for Diamond, believe it. I'll always be from The Gardens but I'm moving, bloop."

"Bloop and bloop. Let's drink."

"Let's."

Diamond went inside and poured two strong cranberry and vodka drinks and made a sandwich she split in two parts. It was a leftover steak from Keith's she had taken from the freezer earlier.

"Girl these drinks are lethal and this sandwich…you cooked this?"

"Nope, my man did. I did add the mayo, tomatoes and bread from Publix."

"Keep his ass cause I'm not a steak person but this is fire."

"Because the steak we ate growing up was thin and tough—this ain't that." Rose screamed with laughter, reminding Diamond of their childhood.

"Damn chuck steak, had to beat it with a mallet and it was still tough, full of textures." Rose said.

"Gristle and that weird little spongy, chewy thing. Mom would be looking at you like you better eat that steak, gristle and all and we did."

The sisters chewed and sipped filled with memories. After their dad disappeared, they moved to The Gardens. Kevin was five, Diamond three and Rose two. Three years later Crystal was born from a relationship Elaine was involved in. Christopher was a good guy who seemed to love Elaine and adored Crystal but was overwhelmed by Elaine's other children. He returned to Nassau, Bahamas where he was from when Crystal was three. Elaine became a lot like Rose was, bitter and reclusive; the difference being she worked two jobs to provide for her four children. Elaine never mentioned Christopher's name again, not even to Crystal.

"Diamond, do you think Crystal ever looked for him? That seems like something she would do."

"If she has, she's never mentioned it. Crys is a move on woman. She doesn't churn and burn about stuff like we do. That's her real strength."

"I bet she will churn and burn if Messiah dips."

"Hell, I'll churn and burn for her because that's a grown ass man who shows his feelings and got all that extra."

Rose held up her cup in acknowledgment.

CHAPTER FIVE

The room was huge and the lighting low. Candles burned; the scent of white sage filled the air. There were two huge tables with sparkling white sheets covering them. Two ancient looking Japanese women stood near the tables. Diamond glanced at Keith. He grinned at her, winking.

"I know you baked a grip of cakes this week and I had three websites so I figured we could get massages, salt scrubs and steam baths— together. These sisters are no joke." Diamond swallowed a lump, she had never in almost thirty-four years had a massage much less this kind of spa experience. "We change to our underwear and get on the table. They handle the rest." The sisters bowed and disappeared from the room. Keith pulled Diamond's face into his hands, kissing first her lips and then her forehead before stepping back, stepping out of his sweats, and standing before her in his boxers.

Lord, he looks too damn good. Them old women better not touch it.

Following suit she undressed and stood before him in ecru lace, panties and bra. Her curves, round belly and cellulite was on full display. His eyes raked over her, and he bit into his lip.

"You're so damn fine woman. That ass and waist ratio is got damn art and those thighs."

He murmured. There was a light knock and he motioned for Diamond to get on the table. He covered her and got on his table and covered himself before saying, 'come in.'

Two hours later Diamond felt like a new woman. She was relaxed and her skin was glowing. Keith asked if she were good.

"I'm great. Thank you."

"I got you. We are driving to Daytona, I got us a nice room and the hotel has great food. It's wine and dine my Diamond day."

I'll be your Diamond. All day and night.

Once they were in the room, Keith took over. He placed her on the bed, removed her clothes slowly, kissing every inch of her. Diamond was purring with pure pleasure by the time he started licking her, nibbling and sucking until she exploded, her screams filling the room. She tried to return the pleasure, but Keith stopped her as he stood, giving her a full view.

"Nah Ma, not yet." He said, grabbing a condom and slowly, sexily sliding it on his thickness. He got on the bed with her and lifted her legs over his shoulders, giving him full access. He slid in a bit and slid slowly out. Diamond hissed and thrust up to meet him and pull him into her wetness.

"Gotdamn then…" he said and thrust fully inside, giving her the magic of his lovemaking. Keith never touched a woman he didn't make it his business to satisfy—but Diamond got that extra, everything he had pent up. Diamond relaxed fully, giving him back all the pleasure he gave her.

"Hey…" Keith said. Diamond was lying on his chest after two sessions of fire lovemaking.

"Hey…"

"You good?"

"I am."

"Me too—Diamond, I need exclusivity, just you and me seeing each other. Could you be into that?"

Everything in Diamond beamed.

"I *am* into that and into you."

Keith moved his head back to look down at her, his eyes revealing how much he was feeling her.

"We are doing this; I like you more than words and the time we've known each other can say. I'm also an honest man and seeing you handle my son was a lot of goodness."

"I know, I'm the same with my girls. I've denied myself—relationships to be about them. It had to be right, it's been wrong enough times."

"That's a word. There's another thing—I'm starving. I hear they have king crab at the restaurant downstairs."

"Let's go then. I can tear up crab in any and all forms."

"You with me until?"

"Sunday morning." He got out of the bed and started doing the cabbage patch, naked. She stared in full admiration.

¥¥¥¥¥

KJ and Keith Sr. arrived at the house at eight pm. Keith Sr. picked him up from school and they had gone shopping, to eat and for a drive. Vera was at the kitchen table eating when they arrived.

"Where y'all been?" She asked.

"Granddad and I went to get new sneakers and we ate at *Big Wings* and then to the country to let me drive." KJ said after kissing Vera's face. He joined her at the table. Keith Sr. grabbed a bottle of water and looked on, leaning against a counter.

"I cooked baked spaghetti." Vera said, chastisement in her voice. It was KJ's favorite.

"It's just eight grandma, we will eat all of that. We bought you something too. I told grandpa he didn't get you that pink purse you wanted for Christmas. He got it now." Vera looked to Keith Sr. and rolled her eyes. He winked before draining his bottle.

"I'm going to change." Sr. said.

"Where's Keith?" Vera asked.

"Dad said don't answer questions about his business grandma." KJ said. Vera nodded; her nose flared a bit. "It's okay because dad never asks your business. It's equal. I'm going to shower, maybe I can beat you in cards later."

"Sounds good. I made cookies."

"Sounds cool."

Vera watched him lope from the room. She got up and went to find Keith Sr. He was sitting on the side of the bed in sweatpants and a t-shirt. She sat beside him.

"KJ is growing up. Sometimes I forget he's sixteen." Vera said, her voice wistful. Her husband draped his arm around her.

"He is. That therapy is helping, and our son is a great dad." Vera nodded in agreement.

"True. Before you know it, he'll be dating."

"I hope so. He has a lot to offer. I'm glad his daddy is. He's done everything a man, father, even a son can do. It's time for him to live."

Vera heard the message Keith Sr, was sending her, loud and clear.

I need something to do. Keith Sr. stays busy and active with his golf buddies, Keith and KJ and I'm sitting around waiting for them to have time for me.

"Vera, maybe you can start playing cards with your friends again or anything else you like. We have time to do what we want. Truth is Keith nor KJ has *needed* us in years. They come because they want to see us, be here."

Man stop reading my mind. I know all of that.

"I know. The food is in the oven, I'm going to get in bed and watch a show. Tell KJ I'll kick his butt in spades tomorrow."

Keith Sr. kissed her softly and pulled her close.

"That sounds great. I love you Vera Walker, you're my favorite wife."

"I'm your only wife Negro." He chuckled from deep in his gut. They had been saying that same thing to each other for almost forty years.

CHAPTER SIX

Diamond held her phone, her mouth hanging open.

"Hello?" The deep feminine voice said.

"I'm sorry, this is Diamond of Diamond's Delights, how can I help you?"

"I'm Cinnamon Black and I want to order your lemon curd and cream cheesecake and your strawberry cream cake please. I need four large Bundt cakes for a meeting I'm hosting."

"Yes ma'am, Mrs. Black, your cake inspired my lemon cake. Why are you buying cakes?"

Diamond asked, truly perplexed. Throaty laughter filled her ears.

"Because no woman can eat only her own cakes. I bake for family and friends only. I utilize local and particularly black-owned businesses at other times. I have eaten your lemon and butter toffee cakes and they are divine." Diamond listened, her heart racing. *Oh my god. That's Cinnamon Black, oh my god, oh my god.* "Please add lots of business cards with my order. You can invoice me at *cblack@cblack.COM*.

She has her own dot.com. Oh my god.

"Yes ma'am. Thank you so much. When do you need the cakes by?"

"I need them Friday at noon. I know it's Monday—

"That's fine. I'll have them there by then. Thank you."

Diamond was nearly hyperventilating when she hung up. Messiah hadn't affected her that way. She recalled reading books and articles by Mrs. Black as a teen and later a young mother. Rose who was finishing up, stared at her.

"Who was that?" Rose asked.

"Mrs. Cinnamon Black just ordered my cakes. She says she loves them." Rose swept the last dust into the pan and dumped it before responding.

"Money is money. You owe me ninety dollars for today."
Diamond didn't expect Rose to understand.

"That's seventy-eight dollars after taxes."
Diamond retorted. Rose held out her hand.

"Cash please."

Diamond reached in her apron pocket and counted out the money, placing it in Rose's hand. Rose recounted it and placed the money, neatly folded in her front pocket.

"Thanks Rose, I'll need you tomorrow also."

"I'll be here. I need a cake now though."

"Get your cake. I need a nap before the girls get home." It was noon, they had started working at six am, only stopping for Diamond to drive the girls to school.

"Umm hmm, all that freaky sex this weekend. No use denying it, you are walking different." Diamond made a face at her sister. "Take a soak and get some rest, I got the girls."

Diamond grabbed Rose, hugging her tightly and kissing all over her face. Rose pushed her away, making a face of disgust.

"Ugh chick, I don't know where them lips been." Diamond poked out her lips.

"All over his…" Rose pulled on her headphones, grabbed her cake and raced from the house.

¥¥¥¥¥

Rose saw Reggie on her porch as she made her way home. She forgot he stopped by on Mondays to chill as he called it. He brought her drinks for the week and bags full of snacks for her and the girls. There were also likely clothes she nor the girls needed.

"How long you been here?" Rose asked. He was wearing all white today and with his skin tone and upper body muscular build, he looked good.

"Bout an hour. I figured you was at Rose's since the car is here."

"Rose hired me to help her. She's paying me." Reggie's brow lifted theatrically. Rose snorted and sat in the chair next to him. The scent of Polo Black cologne tickled her nose. Reggie was the cleanest man she ever met and always smelled good.

"Woman, stop sniffing me. Helping your sister for money, Ro?" He sounded slightly disgusted. Reggie was family over everything and though smart with his money overly generous.

"Don't judge me, Reggie. She asked me and she offered fifteen an hour. Minimum wages are what, nine dollars. She's taking out taxes too."

"That's great she's making bank but man we volunteer with our people." Rose sucked her teeth.

"Reggie, I'm getting what she offered. Now, do you have time for me or what?"

Reggie grinned cockily. He knew Rose needed sexual maintenance at least three times weekly and being in a wheelchair only meant he couldn't walk—he knew he had the other thing on lock. Rose was his first love—

and since the accident, his only. For her once they were together it was always him.

"I got you."

She walked past him inside making sure to touch him. Smiling, he turned his wheelchair around and followed her inside, kicking the door shut. They had two and a half hours before she picked up the kids.

¥¥¥¥¥

Keith watched KJ walk to the truck. He stopped to bump fists with a couple of kids and smiled at a few others.

He's coming into his own. This school of accelerated learning has been great for my son.

"What's up dad?" KJ said, sliding in the vehicle.

"Everything. How are you?"

"I'm good." KJ grinned at his dad, his eyes smiling.

"Good, I need to stop by the mayor's office. I'm signing a two-year contract to update and maintain their websites."

KJ held up his fist for his dad to bump. Keith taught him to celebrate himself and others.

"That's big things."

"It is."

Keith and KJ were sitting in a huge conference room, Keith reading over the papers when Aura Felipe, the mayor's wife and attorney entered with her daughter Amy. Keith stood to shake Aura's hand, but KJ didn't move.

"Keith James you better stand up and shake my Mama's hand." Amy retorted. Keith turned to glance at his son who slowly stood, offering his hand to Aura but stared at Amy. His eyes were hooded, his expression unreadable.

"It's nice to meet you Ms. Felipe. I'm KJ, this is my dad."

"It's my pleasure. Amy told me you assist her with reading music, and she helps you with math." Aura said. Keith was watching his son face was suddenly showing his feelings. He was uncomfortable, KJ was rarely uncomfortable. *It's that girl.* Keith thought. Amy was watching KJ.

"Yes. She's great with math and sings well but her ear for music is very sad." KJ said. Aura laughed and Amy made a face.

"Mr. Walker, your son talks trash to his math tutor, tell him that's not allowed especially

since his trig is even sadder than my ear."
Keith gave Amy his attention.

"I will. Math is important."

"Math is life, but music is love." KJ said. Amy grinned at him.

"Boy, the next time you steal my words, I'm charging you." Amy said. KJ laughed, blushing hard. "Mom, I'm going to see dad, nice meeting you Mr. Walker. KJ, stay out of trouble, if you can, I know it's hard." She left the room and KJ's eyes followed her. Keith was flabbergasted. Not once had KJ mentioned knowing Amy Felipe to him.

"KJ, I heard you just turned sixteen. Happy belated." Aura said.

"Thank you. Amy will be fourteen in February."

"Don't remind me—she already thinks she's thirty."

What is this? My son has a little secret life. He stared at his son who didn't return the look.

"Is everything in the contract to your approval, Mr. Walker?" Aura asked, diverting Keith's attention from KJ.

"Everything is great."

Keith signed the papers. Aura asked him to wait while she got them certified. Keith turned to KJ as soon as she exited the room.

"You have never mentioned knowing Amy Felipe." Keith said.

"Oh, we have tutored each other since school started. She's two years younger but we are in the same grade. She's outspoken but filters better than me. Smart too."

"She's also cute." Keith said. KJ faced his dad, his face serious.

"Amy is beautiful. Her soul is beautiful."

Keith nodded; he had nothing else to say. His son had a crush—and at sixteen knew the beauty of souls and appreciated outspoken girls.

At sixteen I didn't know anything—compared to what my autistic son knows innately.

"Amy is very young." Keith said once they were in the car.

"Dad, she is my friend—friend. I'm very young also. What do you tell me?"

"Which thing do I tell you?"

"Do not make a thing out of nothing. That's *your* advice."

Keith's mouth opened and closed. *Did he just use me against me?*

"It is good advice." Keith said lamely.

"KJ is following it."

"I see you, Keith James."

KJ pointed from Keith's eyes to his before pulling on his headphones.

Most folks think he's Keith Jr. Amy calls him Kevin James. I am not ready.

¥¥¥¥¥

After KJ was in bed Keith phoned Diamond. He wanted to hear her voice after a sexy and fun weekend. She encouraged him to ride the Ferris wheel at Daytona Beach. He hadn't been on a Ferris wheel in over twenty years. He told her about KJ.

"That's so cute."

"Don't say cute. I said Amy was cute. He told me and sounded hard, "she's beautiful and her soul is beautiful.""

"Oh, KJ has game. Wonder where he got that from."

"Not my ass. That's all him. I mean I got a Lil something, but beautiful soul is him."

"You got a lot and he's paying attention to you. Guess who's delivering cakes to Mrs. Cinnamon Black Friday."

"Hmm, tasty cakes?" Keith asked and Diamond's vibrant laughter caressed his ears.

"Diamond's Delights, nobody wants tasty when they can be delighted." She said saucily.

"That's fo sho and your real delights they don't even know." His groin tightened, thinking of her delights.

"And they won't. I got cakes baking, come get it tomorrow—

"The cake or you?"

"We can do a two for one. About noon."

"Bet."

Diamond's Delights is right. She named that just right. She has become Keith's delight.

CHAPTER SEVEN

At exactly noon Keith knocked on Diamond's door. She tried to hurry and answer it, but Rose was closer.

"I see why you've been trying to rush me home." Rose said, walking in with Keith. "Computer man was coming to get some— cake. I see everything about you Diamond Diane Moore." Diamond waved her off but didn't quite meet Rose's eyes.

"Diamond Diane, you didn't tell your sister your man was coming at noon. Should I feel dissed?" Keith asked moving closer to Diamond.

"It didn't come up Keith Walker."

Rose was propped up on the broom watching them.

"I need to be acknowledged. I want you saying, "My mans is coming at noon." He said in a sad version of a girl. Diamond started giggling.

"Don't mind me, I'm going to just put away the broom and leave." Rose said. Neither of them acknowledged her. "Diamond!" Frowning Diamond looked around Keith at Rose.

"Rose!"

"Girl stop playing, I need my money." Rose said, holding her hand out. Diamond took the money from her pocket, slapping it in Rose's hand. Rose slowly counted it to aggravate her sister.

"Great, I'll see you later. Take your time here, I'll get the girls. We are going to see a show and get some food. You got until six." Rose said and sauntered out.

"We've got five hours." Keith said.

"You got that kind of time?" Diamond asked. She felt jittery with the way Keith was staring at her. Her nipples hardened, showing through her t-shirt. Keith's eyes slid over them.

"Yea, I work for me." She grabbed his hand and led him to her room.

"Undress." She said. Keith didn't hesitate, he slowly undressed for her until he stood before her naked. Diamond walked into his arms and started kissing him and slowly worked her way down his body until she was on her knees in front of him. Keith gritted his teeth against the desire to ravish her. She looked up at him sexily before taking him in her mouth and slowly savoring him. He tried to keep his eyes open, but it felt so good his eyes closed. Otherwise, he would have exploded in her throat.

He finally pulled away lifting her. He pulled her shirt over her head with the bra. Her breast sprung free, her chocolate nipples hard. Leaning in he grabbed one between his teeth and nibbled.

"Ooooo." Diamond uttered. Keith moved to the other nipple working his magic there. "Keith—please."

"Please what, Baby?"

"Please get inside me before I lose my mind." Her voice sounded rough. Keith slid his hand inside the waist of her pants and pulled them down. Red lace panties enhanced her curves.

"Lose your mind? Look at you—it's my mind that's wrecked."

Diamond backed slowly away and fell on the bed, pulling her panties down. Keith groaned deep in his chest before covering her on the bed, pushing her legs open and pushing inside—hard. "Let's lose our minds."

¥¥¥¥¥

At five fifteen Keith prepared to leave.

"I am seriously feeling you, Diamond." He said at the door.

"We are." They were being cautious about saying love, yet.

"I need you to meet my folks." Her eyes widened. Meeting the folks was serious. He had met the girls, Crystal and Rose and she met KJ, but the parents were more. "Yes Diamond. I'm going to say Sunday, but I'll let you know. The girls are invited too."

"If I'm doing this, let it just be me for the first time." Her eyes searched his for understanding. Though Keith was a single dad she knew people judged single moms more harshly. She needed to test the waters before exposing the girls.

"That's fair. I'll let you know. Diamond—this feels damn good." His intensity excited and unnerved her.

"It does. Call me."

"You know I will." He kissed her thoroughly before leaving. They both wanted him to stay.

I'm falling in love. Keith thought.

I might be in love. Diamond mused.

At six pm the girls arrived in a cloud of noise with bags full of junk food and other stuff from Rose. Diamond was glad because she was going to order pizza.

"Mom, we ate at the movie theatre." Emerald said. "The Center City theatre has food and wine. TT only had one wine. We then went to the candy and popcorn store. TT said you paid for everything."

I guess I did. Rose could care less about the money.

"Mom, why you look like that?" Opal asked suspiciously. She touched Diamond's forehead.

"Like what?"

"All dreamy. Mom you're getting weird. You aren't even fussing about us eating junk."

"Just a little tired and hungry. I was going to order pizza but since y'all ate I'll make a sandwich." Opal stared at her several seconds before going to her room. Emerald sat on the footstool near Diamond's chair.

"I'm glad you aren't fussing mom, it's a good look."

"Thanks, I think."

"You're welcome. Having a business and a boyfriend is good for you. That's what TT said. I agree."

"Do you now?"

"Yes ma'am. You're the best mom but you were grumpy—a lot. Now you smile and look dreamy. That's good. I can make you a sandwich." Diamond tweaked Emerald's nose.

"I would like that. I want turkey, lots of tomatoes and a tiny bit of mayo."

"I got you—just chill."

When Emerald returned with the sandwich, Diamond was asleep. She covered her and took the sandwich to the refrigerator. She got on the sofa across from her mom and opened the latest *rebel girl's* book. Her and Amber were reading them together.

¥¥¥¥¥

KJ was home when Keith arrived.

"Hey dad, what you want to eat?"

"I'm starving, let's order pizza. You didn't go to dad and mom's?"

"No, dad I'm sixteen. I want the *MEATZA* pizza. What you want?" The I'm sixteen comment didn't go over Keith's head. KJ had been catching the bus to his grandparents for years if Keith was busy. The bus came to their home as well.

"I'll take the same, you better get two. I know you're sixteen son—I also know you can take care of yourself." Keith said.

"I did my homework and my laundry. I'm going to order the pizza. Might as well get wings too."

"Might as well. I'm going to shower."

Keith phoned Vera once he was in his room.

"Hey mom, y'all good?"

"We are. What's up with you and my baby?"

"He's ordering pizza and I'm getting ready to chill with him. I called to ask if I can bring Diamond to meet you and dad Sunday." There was a brief pause, but Vera said, "of course. Will the kids be coming?"

"Not this time. Thanks mom, tell dad I'll call him tomorrow."

"I will."

Vera hung up and faced Keith Sr. who was watching her.

"That was Keith, he's bringing his lady friend by on Sunday."

"Great. Can't wait to meet her." Vera glanced away from his gaze, and he picked up his newspaper. Earlier she had fussed because KJ called to say he was going home.

During dinner Keith asked KJ if he would be going to his grandparents less.

"Some days I want to go and do things with granddad and play cards with grandma and somedays I want to come home. At home I can eat what I want, watch sports, do music or draw. I need more time like that Dad." The younger man watched his dad as he spoke. Keith realized for all his honesty and bluntness there were things KJ had learned not to say. They were the things he needed to say such as what he wanted to do.

"I like that. Come home as much as you want. That's why we have our own spaces here. I know some days playing cards and watching *The Price Is Right* reruns is a lot." KJ snorted because he didn't like game shows.

"Bruh, a lot. Thanks dad, you're the best."

"I'm taking Diamond to meet mom and dad Sunday. The girls aren't coming, do you want to be there?"

"No thanks. I'm good on that." KJ said so drily Keith almost choked with laughter. KJ's expression of thanks but no thanks cracked Keith up even more.

"I hear you son I do. Now let's see what this college ball looks like." KJ did a swoosh move with his hands.

CHAPTER EIGHT

Diamond stared at herself in the car mirror before getting out. She decided to wear her specially designed cake chef clothing. It was like a traditional chef's outfit but hers were brown or pink and embossed with her logo. Today she wore the brown one. She invited Rose to come with her, but she quickly declined.

"I don't do bougie. Your bout as bougie as I can take." Rose said before saluting her sister and leaving.

Cinnamon Black opened the door to the small house and grabbed Diamond in an embrace, startling her.

"I'm a hugger honey. Do you need help with the cakes?"

Diamond's heart was thumping in her chest. Cinnamon didn't seem quite real to her. In person she was quite tall, and elegance oozed from her pores, but her smile, eyes and hug were genuine and warm. She was dressed in black and pearls, but her shoes were leather converses and she smelled great.

"No ma'am. I have a rolling cart. I just wanted to make sure someone was here, I'm a bit early. You smell better than my cakes." Cinnamon giggled, her eyes twinkling with humor.

121

"It's *Fucking Fabulous.*"

"Ma'am?" Diamond asked, unsure what she heard.

"The perfume is named *Fucking Fabulous.* It's by Tom Ford. It's my favorite. Let's get those cakes."

Oh my, she's fucking fabulous. Diamond thought as she got her cart, filled it with the four huge cakes and rolled it inside. She was surprised to see twenty teens inside.

"Hello girls, this is Ms. Diamond Moore, she owns *Diamond's Delights* cakes. They are fabulous. Diamond these young entrepreneurs are my mentees. We talk about education, life, careers and boys sometimes. Do you have time to join us?"

Diamond looked around the beautiful room and at the girls all staring at her expectantly.

"I do."

"Then join us for cake, tea and conversation."

Cinnamon talked to the girls and Diamond listened as intently as they did. She invited Diamond to talk about her business.

"In short, I was a single mom with two daughters who was known for her cakes. I never allowed myself to think of having a business. I sold them to make extra money but a year ago I was offered fifty dollars for a cake. After that cake more people wanted cakes and I earned enough to pay my bills and save. Just a few months ago my sister, younger sister Crystal encouraged me to incorporate my business and today I'm here. Now I believe in myself and my business. I'm almost thirty-four. My daughter Opal who is thirteen designed my logo. By the summer my goal is to have a cake truck. There is nothing like owning yourself." Cinnamon stood and started clapping and the girls joined her.

"Ms. Black thanks so much for today." Diamond said at the door.

"You're welcome. My young ladies need to hear from real life entrepreneurs. Everyone isn't corporate. I encourage having your own business even as a side gig. Thank you for being so spontaneous. Those cakes were so delicious. You're a cake goddess."

Diamond hugged Cinnamon impulsively and found herself once again in a cocoon of warmth and beautiful scent.

"I'll have a huge order soon. I'll give you ample time. Congratulations—consider yourself family, your sister is my son's boo."

Diamond was close to wringing her hands. She wasn't one to fangirl, but Cinnamon Black inspired it. That day confirmed it.

"Yes ma'am. Thanks again. I've got a twelve-cake order waiting on me."

"Go and be great."

Diamond beamed all the way home.

I'm taking my books to be signed next time.

Once she was home Diamond phoned Crystal, almost hyperventilating.

"Girl, I know. She's so kind and real. She set me up with Messiah after talking to me for ten minutes. She feels energy."

I'm glad Rose didn't go because that energy of hers. Diamond thought and snickered. She didn't say that to Crystal because as mean as Rose was to Crystal, she didn't like others saying anything about her.

"I'm thanking her for Keith too because one thing led to the next thing."

"Claim it then!" Crystal said.

"Yessss!"

¥¥¥¥¥

The last cakes were out of the oven when Keith arrived. The girls were with Crystal. Messiah had flown to New York for a one-night performance and Crystal asked for the girls to come for a girls night.

Keith wrapped his arms around her as soon as she opened the door.

"That's the second great hug today." She said. Keith pulled back, staring down at her.

"I need more information. I'm assuming the girls hug you daily." His expression was inscrutable.

"Man, I was hugged by Ms. Black. She gives great hugs." Diamond watched his expression change into a sexy grin.

"That I understand. She's known for her hugs. I was ready to start capping anyone who was hugging on you. I'm not a jealous man but I don't want you getting *great* hugs unless it's your people. Ms. C is the exception."

"Ms. C, you know her like that?"

"I know Muhammad and Messiah like that which means she checks you out and embraces you if she's feeling you."

"Crystal said she embraces energy."

"That's it exactly. She will love you and check you. Her and her husband. We eating cake?" He asked sniffing the air.

"Funny, I told you I was cooking. There's chicken roasting and I cooked cabbage and cornbread."

Keith patted his belly.

"That's what's up. Beautiful, talented, sexy and my baby can cook. I see everything you bringing."

Diamond started doing a bop and a drop. Keith watched her and realized he hadn't seen her dance. To match her, he got closer and bopped too. Diamond moved closer, grinding and bopping, changing the temperature in the room. She screamed with joy when Keith did the sexiest grind and bop, she had ever seen.

"What Diamond Moore, you ain't know I could grind and bop?"

"Not with your clothes on!"

He started grinding slower and closer. Diamond felt everything he was giving, big D, sexy energy. The only music was the beat in their heads and watching each other. A knock on the door stopped then in mid-grind.

"Who in the hell…" Diamond muttered as she walked to the door, Keith on her heels. It was Rose with a cup in her hand.

131

"Oh shit, your man here. Why y'all sweating like that?" Rose asked, sniffing the air. Keith grinned at her antics.

"We were dancing." Diamond said.

"I don't hear any music." Rose said, peeking inside as if she were looking for the music. Keith stood behind Diamond, close

"Rose." Diamond said, her voice annoyed.

"Fine, just hand me a cake and I can smell chicken roasting and I *know* you cooked two, so I want half of one. I'll then take my unwelcome self home." Diamond sucked her teeth but invited her in. Keith sat in an armchair and Rose on the loveseat. "Rose behave."

"I'm the bad sister." Rose said to Keith. "My man is an ex-drug boy; I don't work and have almost zero ambition. They're always telling me to act right. There's no fun in that."

Keith laughed uproariously at Rose's words, surprising her.

"Do you lil Sis. If you're cool with you, I'm cool with you." He said. Diamond rushed back in with a pan of food.

"See how she damn near ran in here. Scared I'm going to say something bad. Thanks Diamond. Keith, you're okay with me. Later." Rose said as she waltzed from the room.

"Rose is a live one." Keith said.

"The understatement of the year. I'm hungry."

"Me too." Keith said.

¥¥¥¥¥

"Baby, you cook like somebody's grandma and that's the highest compliment." Keith said after eating more than half a chicken, a pile of cabbage and cornbread.

"Elaine had me cooking early. I was the cook, Rose the cleaner, I'm telling you, you can eat off Rose's floors. Kevin as the son did nothing around the house but at fifteen, he was working and bringing home groceries. Crystal was the baby and much younger than all of us, but she did a little of everything, very little. She was my baby too and I had her focus on the books."

"I love that, a family playing to their strengths. I did it all as the only child except cook—Vera didn't want that, but I taught myself to burn a little. My dad grills a little and fries fish. I've never had roasted chicken like that."

"The secret is garlic and butter under the skin and olive oil on the skin for crispness and my own magic."

"You're damn sure magical. I rub your icing on my body…"

Diamond's eyes narrowed at the idea of Keith with icing on his big, hard body.

"Why you ogling me?" Keith asked, his voice lowered.

"I'm thinking of covering you with icing and licking it off—slowly. Real slowly."

A groan escaped his throat at how she said it and the image it created in his mind. His erection grew.

"That's so damn—

"Oh it will be. You're my chocolate cake and I've got lemon buttercream icing. I'm going to need all that food you ate to settle though."

"Smart woman because cabbage makes me gassy." He said and Diamond wrinkled her nose.

"Yup, I'll wait."

"You are love woman. I want you to know that." She winked at him, but the L word didn't go unnoticed. She had never felt as free with a man—anyone if she was being completely honest.

"Can you stay?"

"Try to make me leave. KJ is with my folks. I am picking him up tomorrow though. He's reminded me lately he's sixteen."

"Ms. Opal is thirteen and thinks she and Emerald can stay here alone. That is not happening, she will be eighteen before that occurs. I don't care what kids think honestly. They are kids—period until they aren't. I remember being sixteen when Kevin went in the service and was home alone with fifteen-year-old Rose and ten-year-old Crystal. I was petrified. In my mind you aren't grown until you're grown." Keith nodded in agreement. He was seventeen and a senior before being left alone at home at night. He wanted to earlier but even Keith Sr. wasn't with that.

"I'm with you. I must admit I need to give KJ more space. When he came to live with me, he was struggling, and it took a few years to work that out. Then there's the speaking without filtering thing which made me very protective. I realized the other day he filters a lot more than I realized. We are both in therapy to deal with that but he's a good young'un who deserves more space. In fact, I allowed him to make the basement his own space this week. It has a bedroom, bath and a living area. The laundry room is down there too. He loves it."

"You're a great dad Keith and a damn good man."

"Having an autistic son with a runaway mom grew me up. Ten years ago, I was an out in them streets twenty-seven-year-old. Being a full-time dad manned me up. As a single mom at twenty you know that, but men are slower."

"That's the damn good part, many men and women stay children even once they have children. I respect you, a lot."

Keith's heart felt the word respect. His dad used to tell him, *"the Bible never tells a woman to love her husband but to respect him. It commands a man to love his wife. But if she respects you, she will love you."*

"That's high praise Diamond. I need a nap."

"A nap sounds great."

They slept wrapped around each other until two am—they woke, showered and Diamond got the icing.

CHAPTER NINE

Diamond changed clothes three times before going to dinner at Keith's parents. She insisted on driving herself. When she walked out in the third outfit Rose who was there, and Opal had enough.

"Mom, you seriously looked great in everything. Just stop." Opal said.

"Thanks Opal because they are just people. Keith likes you, his son likes you, so bump those people." Rose added.

Emerald ever the peacemaker said, "Mom, this *is* the best look. You can never go wrong with a black jumpsuit. You look beautiful and your new hair-color is fire."

Diamond's huge curly fro was praline colored and it was perfect with her skin and the loose-fitting jumpsuit she splurged on. She allowed Rose to makeup her face, lightly. She was *not* a makeup person like Rose was and Opal aspired to.

"For real." Rose said.

"Okay, okay." Diamond said. "This is it. I'm going. Rose, y'all staying here or going to your house?"

"Here, you got cakes. Reggie taking the girls to school in the morning. I might even spend the night."

"I'll believe that when I see it." Diamond said and rose chuckled. Rose only wanted to sleep in her own bed. On the rare occasion she went to a hotel she took her own sheets and pillows.

¥¥¥¥¥

Keith was getting out of his car when Diamond pulled in next to him. When she got out, he whistled, making her blush hard. He pulled her into an embrace once he was close to her.

"You look so hot; did you bring that icing?" He whispered.

"Keith Walker, we are proper in this space." Keith backed off, holding up his hands.

"Okay but I'll never forget how you iced me."

"Nor should you because I will ice you again because your response to being iced is something I'll never forget." They didn't see Vera staring out the blinds. Keith Sr. gently pulled her away.

"Let's go inside before I…"

Diamond walked ahead of him and pressed the buzzer. Vera opened the door almost immediately a smile posted on her face.

"Hello Diamond, welcome." She said.

"Thank you."

Keith Sr. spoke and embraced her.

"Welcome Diamond."
Diamond was startled by how much Keith and KJ favored Keith Sr.

"Thank you."

Vera led them to the living room which was nice but over furnished.

"Diamond, I hear you're the cake lady." Sr. said.

"Sir, I'm a baker. I love it. My grandma taught me and that became my thing. It now pays my bills." Diamond said. Keith's eyes were on her, a big smile on his face.

"My wife and I were custodians. I was a supervisor, but we cleaned for a living. We never considered being entrepreneurs. I'm glad for y'all. You and my son work for yourselves and doing good." Sr. said. Vera's face flushed and Keith smiled at his dad. Keith Sr. always came through.

"My sister Rose isn't a custodian, but she could be. She is the Clean Queen."

"There's good money in owning a cleaning business." Sr. said.

"It's hard work." Vera said. "And can be nasty."

"My mom once cleaned motel rooms, she said that was the nastiest, but she had kids to feed." Diamond said.

"Speaking of feeding, I roasted chicken." Vera said. "I figured everyone loves chicken, there's also greens, sweet potatoes and rolls."

"Sounds great." Diamond said.

The dinner was good, and Diamond said that.

"Diamond adds garlic and butter to her roasted chicken." Keith said. Vera and Diamond shot him a look. He looked completely unaware of their looks. Keith Sr. held back a smile.

"I don't care for garlic." Vera said. He glanced at Diamond who was giving him face. Keith Sr. looked on in approval.

"It's great either way." Keith said. Sr. chuckled and got a look from his wife. Dessert was peach cobbler; Diamond ate two servings.

"That peach cobbler was delicious. I don't even try with pies and cobblers; something always goes wrong. I would love some to go." Diamond said. For the first time since they arrived Vera smiled, genuinely.

"For sure."

They stayed an hour after dinner, Keith Sr. and Diamond doing most of the talking. Keith sat as close to Diamond as was decent.

"Where is KJ?" Vera asked as they prepared to leave.

"He's at the house." Keith said. "He's reminding me he's sixteen now. I allowed him to have his own space in the basement."

Vera's mouth tightened.

"I need to come see that space." Keith Sr. said. "A man needs that."

"What did he eat?" Vera asked.

"Mom, I cooked a meal for him." Keith said. Diamond touched his arm which did not go unnoticed by Vera or Keith Sr.

She's good for him. Sr. thought. Vera wanted to smack him.

"Keith, I know you cook." Keith didn't respond. Diamond's hand on his arm tempered him.

151

"I love y'all." He said instead.

"Thanks Mr. and Mrs. Walker." Diamond said.

"Are you okay?" Keith asked at Diamond's car.

"The question Keith is are you okay? There was some kind of strange vibe with you and your mom and mentioning how I cook my chicken didn't help." A look of pure bewilderment rested on Keith's face.

"I'm confused. I simply said you added butter and garlic to your chicken, what's strange about that?"

"Keith no mom or woman really wants a comparison of their food, especially a mom. You might not have meant it as a comparison but that's how your mom took it."

"Cool, I'll own that even if I didn't mean it that way. However, I know my mom and she's a control freak, she doesn't think I can feed my son properly or because he's autistic he should ever be alone. If it were up to Vera Walker, my son and I would live with her. She would prepare our meals, do our laundry and tell us how to live our lives. Knowing her as *I* do I have to say certain things to avoid all that. Diamond, you're here as my woman and no one, not my mom or dad or KJ for that matter gets a vote on that. Please don't take that on. I got this. Just be with me and love me as your man and I'll do the same for you in the presence of your people." He said with a certain amount of force and Diamond heard —and understood him. All her life, her role had been to run interference.

"You're right, I should have just eaten the dry chicken and said nothing.

"You can always speak but yes on the dry chicken." He said. They both busted out laughing. Vera roasted chicken breasts without skin, and they were a bit dry.

"The greens and peach cobbler were excellent."

"They always are. She should have cooked oxtail or short ribs and you would have licked your plate. We got to know our strengths."

"I hear you. So, I'm supposed to love you, huh?"

Keith held up crossed fingers.

"That's the plan and I'm going to love you with everything in me. On word." He pulled her close and kissed her forehead. "I'm going home to watch football with the son, what's your plan?"

"Sunday evening nap. I'm sending Rose home and getting in my bed. The girls nap too on Sundays. I'll call you when I wake up."

"I'll be waiting." He said and kissed her again. He watched her drive away before walking back to his parents' door and knocking. Vera answered.

"Mom, Diamond will be my wife one day and KJ's stepmom." Vera didn't say anything but nodded. Keith gave her a hug before walking to his car and driving away. Sr. walked up behind Vera and placed his arms around her.

"Vera, she's a good one. Keith is already in love with her and her with him. You and I got married two months after we met."

"Man, I know that. Was my chicken good?"

"Woman, your chicken is always good. Let's go snuggle."

Vera knew exactly what snuggle meant and Sr. was an excellent snuggler.

¥¥¥¥¥

Everything for the game was set up when Keith arrived home. There were their favorite snacks, beer for Keith in an ice bucket and a sprite for KJ. He didn't drink caffeinated drinks.

"Man, you are the real MVP." Keith said, dropping into his lounger.

"You taught me. How was dinner?"

"It was good. Son, I'm falling in love with Diamond." Keith said.

"I hope so. She's a nice lady and she's really pretty. Her kids are good too; Opal a little extra but Ms. Diamond watches her good. Emerald will be a great little sister."

Okay then.

"Dad, you need a good lady. That chicken you brought home was bomb." Keith started laughing hard. "I guess grandma cooked her chicken, huh?" Keith almost slid out of his chair, laughing. "Everybody should not bake chicken. She should have cooked short ribs." Keith rushed from the room, laughing so hard he had to pee.

Diamond, you are right. KJ is just fine as he is. He sees all of us as we are and loves us anyway.

"Dad, you good?"

"Never better son. Let's see what these Jaguars trying to do."

"Lose, I'm thinking." That set Keith off again. The Jaguars record was seriously bad.

¥¥¥¥¥

Diamond woke up with both girls in her bed. Emerald was asleep but Opal was staring at her.

"What?" Diamond asked.

"Are you in love or something?"

"Almost."

"Okay, that's why you're acting so weird. TT said he's a good man. If TT approves, he must be cause TT don't like people like that. I like him even if his kid is a pain." Diamond grabbed her oldest and squeezed her tightly.

Opal pretended not to like it but snuggled closer.

"TT is right on this. You hungry?" Diamond asked.

"TT cooked crabs with everything in them. There's crabs, corn, potatoes and sausage in the refrigerator. Her crabs are the best." Diamond sat up and stretched before getting out of bed.

"They are. I'm going to get some, you coming?"

"Yes ma'am. We going to let Em sleep?"

"Until she wakes up. Let's go." They knew Emerald didn't like being woken up. She often said her brain renewed while she slept. Diamond was also aware Opal liked time alone with her even if she didn't ask for it.

They quietly got out of bed. Diamond went to wash up and Opal went to get things ready.

CHAPTER TEN

After several weeks of assisting Diamond with her business Rose asked her sister how hard it was to start a business. Diamond was startled by the question but made sure not to show it. They were so busy they hired one of the girls Cinnamon mentored as a paid intern.

"Why?"

They were on Diamond's porch having cocktails after an exhausting week.

"Damn it woman, answer the question." Rose responded.

"Starting it is easy. You chose a name, register your business, talk to an attorney on certain things. The work is the hard part."

"I'm thinking of cleaning houses and apartments. I'm good at it and Reggie thinks it's a great idea. I cleaned a place for his friend, and they paid me four hundred dollars for six hours. I know every place won't pay that but that's sixty-six dollars an hour." Diamond wanted to jump off the porch and race around the neighborhood but played it cool.

"That's good money, everyone won't pay that, but you set your prices. I can help you with registering and stuff."

"Cool, I'm in the thinking stage so don't get all excited and start posting on the internet or calling it *The Sexiest Maid* or something."

"I wouldn't dare. I don't need you embarrassing me by saying I'm lying. Who needs that?"

"Whatever. Just stick a pin in it. I got another place to clean tomorrow for the same amount."

She's going to do it. I'm going to wait her little ass out.

"Whenever, it's not like I have nothing to do. Forty cakes a week, moving in six weeks and a man. Whatever is right?"

"Diamond, you ain't fooling me. You can't wait until I say go."

"Heffa, I got a whole life and your business ain't it."

"Stop lying. You want it for all of us. Feel free to tell *your* sister." Rose said. Diamond rolled her eyes theatrically. She would tell Crystal once it was a thing because she knew her sister, she would start rounding up houses for

Rose to clean and that would become a thing. The next move would be on Rose.

I finally do have a whole life and I'm living it.

EPILOGUE

The Diamond Moore house as the sign out front indicated was move-in ready. Diamond, her girls, Keith, KJ and Crystal stood out front staring at it. Crystal moved into her new home three weeks earlier.

"This is beautiful Di. I'm so happy for you." Crystal said. "Girls, what do you think?"

"It's beautiful." They said in unison.

"I have a question." KJ said. Keith immediately alerted. When KJ alerted you about a question it could go either way.

"What's that KJ?" Diamond asked.

"Will this be our second home once dad asks you to marry him and you say yes?" Everyone stared at him except Keith, he stared at Diamond, whose mouth opened and closed twice. She hadn't seen that coming even from KJ.

"KJ, are you proposing on behalf of your dad?" Diamond asked lightly.

"I'm not sure if I can but I would because somebody got to step up."

"KJ." Keith warned.

"What dad? You're in love with her, she's in love with you and y'all getting older every day. Opal shook her head, Crystal held in the laughter that was threatening to explode. This was her second time meeting KJ, and she was as enamored as Diamond.

"Son, please let me handle this. When Diamond and I decide our future, we will then discuss houses and everything. The two of us. Is that okay?" KJ shrugged.

"Sure. I just thought it needed asking and saying. Adults waste a lot of time not saying stuff, that's all."

"KJ, you say the most." Emerald said. "But— your heart is in the right place. Come on inside, there is a fourth bedroom."

"I'm going with the kids." Crystal said.

"What do you think of what KJ said?" Keith asked. His hands were in his pockets, his expression serious.

"I think he said what he feels." Diamond answered cagily.

"Okay, I'll ask this then is that something you would consider?"

"I'll let you know when we get there Keith Walker. Now come on let's go inside with the kids."

"With *our* kids." Keith said and grabbed her hand.

I'm on no hurry. It took me almost thirty-four years to get here. I'm enjoying the journey. Diamond thought.

Thank you, son, for introducing that to the conversation. Keith thought. *You really are the best of me.*

More from the Moore Sisters and their men in 2022

#JustLOVE and Happy New Year!

www.ingramcontent.com/pod-product-compliance
Lightning Source LLC
Chambersburg PA
CBHW052008150726

47999CB00004B/1574